# Nature CAT ™ BREEZY RIDER

**BuzzPop**

# BuzzPop

an imprint of Little Bee Books

New York, NY

Adapted by Diane Muldrow

Copyright © 2021 by Spiffy Entertainment,
LLC. Nature Cat® and associated characters,
trademarks and design elements are owned
by Spiffy Entertainment, LLC. All rights
are reserved to Spiffy Entertainment, LLC,
including the right of reproduction in whole
or in part in any form.
BuzzPop and associated colophon are
trademarks of Little Bee Books.
For more information about
special discounts on bulk purchases,
please contact Little Bee Books at
sales@littlebeebooks.com.
Manufactured in China   RRD 1220
First Edition
10  9  8  7  6  5  4  3  2 1
ISBN 978-1-4998-1094-3 (paperback)
ISBN 978-1-4998-0340-2 (ebook)
buzzpopbooks.com

**Zip! Whoosh!** Three kites darted into the wind. Higher and higher, they flew—looking a lot like Nature Cat and his friends!

"Tally ho! Ha *ha!* Onward and *yonward*!" called Nature Cat from the ground. The kites swirled and twirled.

"Windy days are certainly perfect for kite flying," Daisy declared as her bunny kite soared.

"I know!" said Hal. "It must be because windy days are so windy!"

Squeeks appeared. "Here I am!" she called. "I got my kite! What do I do?"

"Just put your back to the wind," Daisy told Squeeks. "Now wait for a gust . . . and let your kite go!"

"Hmm, ok," said Squeeks. She held out her kite, ready to try. Suddenly, a flurry of wind swept up Squeeks's kite . . .

*. . . along with Squeeks!*

"Not on my watch, Squeeks!" cried Nature Cat, leaping to grab her kite's string.

ut now it was Nature Cat's turn to get pulled up into the air . . .
hen Hal's, then Daisy's!

We'll have you down in a jiffy, Squeeks!" called Nature Cat.

uddenly—**snap!**—the kite's string broke!
Down plunged Squeeks's friends,
ight into a bush.

"No!" Squeeks cried as she blew away from her friends.

With all her strength, Squeeks climbed up the kite tail. . . .

. . . up onto the kite's frame.

"Whoa! Go, Squeeks!" she cheered for herself. "Good job, little mouse!"

Without the string, Squeeks's kite had become a hang glider! Squeeks shifted her weight from side to side, steering it through the air.

"Look, I'm flying!" she cried.

But the fun didn't last long.

# Crash!

Squeeks came to a sudden, leafy stop.

"Well, I *was* flying," she said. "But now, I'm stuck in this tree. On an island. Alone. *HELP!*"

"Fear not, Squeeks!" called Nature Cat. "We'll save you!" He turned to his friends. "But the question is—how can we get to Squeeks?"

"It's certainly too far to swim," Daisy pointed out.

"A taxi?" suggested Hal. "No wait, a skateboard! No wait, a monster truck!"

Just then—**whissshhh!**—the wind blew a leaf across the lake.

"A-ha!" said Nature Cat. "Maybe the wind can push *us* across the water, too!"

"Let's build a sailboat!" suggested Daisy, pulling up a picture on her smartphone. "Wind certainly got Squeeks into this predicament, and now wind will get her out of it!"

In a flash, Daisy tied together wooden logs to make a raft that could float.

Nature Cat added a tiller and rudder for steering the boat.

Together, the friends built a mast to hold the sail.

Hal brought his frog friend, Gregory, for moral support.
"Gregory says we're doing a great job," Hal said.
"But he's wondering what we're going to use for a sail."

"Hey!" said Daisy, hopping to her kite she left on the grass. "Remember how the wind caught our kites and pushed them through the air?"

"Great idea, Daisy!" exclaimed Nature Cat. "Let's turn our kites into a sail!"

He and Daisy quickly taped the three kites together and attached their nice, big sail to the mast. The boat was ready!

"Hear ye, hear ye!" announced Nature Cat as the sail billowed in the cool breeze. "I christen our sailboat, *Breezy Rider*."

"So, um—how do we move?" asked Hal.

"We've got to catch the wind in the sail," Daisy said as the shipmates boarded the boat. "Which way is the wind blowing?"

Hal tossed a leaf into the air, and it flew right back into his face.

"Looks like the wind is coming from over there!" said Hal.

Nature Cat turned the sail until it caught a wind gust.
The boat began to glide.

"Ride, *Breezy Rider*, ride!" called Nature Cat.

Meanwhile, Squeeks was in big trouble! Nevin and Kevin, two hungry owls, found her and put her in a cage.

She needed to escape fast!

She climbed up and out of the cage and ran for some bushes. That's where she found her kite that had fallen to the ground!

The owls swooped down after her. Squeeks grabbed her kite and used it to scare the owls. **"RAWWR!"** she growled like a big, ferocious beast.

"Ah! Let's get out of here, Kevin!" Nevin said.

"Sure thing, Nevin!" Kevin squawked as they quickly fluttered away.

*Breezy Rider* neared the shore.
"Squeeks!" Nature Cat called.

"Nature Cat!" Squeeks shrieked
and let go of her kite.

Suddenly, the owls realized they had been tricked and swooped back down to capture Squeeks.

*Breezy Rider* blew closer to the island. Squeeks leaped . . .

. . . right into Hal's arms.

"Got ya, Squeeks! Ol' buddy, ol' pal!" cried Hal.

"I'll serve some justice to those owls, Nature Cat style," Nature Cat cried. "Tally ho!"

Nature Cat then turned the sail, caught the owls in it, and spun them off into the sky!

"We're really flying now, Kevin!" said Nevin as they soared away.

"Thanks for coming to get me, you guys!" Squeeks said.

Nature Cat felt the wind rush through his whiskers. "Anything for you, Squeeks!" he said, spinning the sail around. "Now whattya say we enjoy this windy day?"

The sail caught the wind—**ploof!**—and *Breezy Rider* began coasting off into the sunset.

"Ha ha ha!" cried Nature Cat. "Onward and *yonward*!"